Christmas *in* Maine

WRITTEN BY
ROBERT P. TRISTRAM COFFIN

WOODBLOCK PRINTS BY
BLUE BUTTERFIELD

FOR KEVIN, SATCHEL, AND BRYCE,
Happiness may write a blank page, but apparently
it still allows you to carve wood.
—BLUE BUTTERFIELD

Islandport Press
PO Box 10
247 Portland Street
Yarmouth, Maine 04096
www.islandportpress.com
books@islandportpress.com

ISBN: 978-1-939017-76-5
Library of Congress Card Number: 2014959693
Dean L. Lunt, Publisher

ISLANDPORT PRESS

Christmas *in* Maine

WRITTEN BY
ROBERT P. TRISTRAM COFFIN

WOODBLOCK PRINTS BY
BLUE BUTTERFIELD

ISLANDPORT  PRESS

FOREWORD

When you read *Christmas in Maine*, you might feel as though Robert P. Tristram Coffin's Christmas existed in a past that never was. How many of us today are lucky enough to live on a saltwater farm—with bays on both sides of it, no less? And how many of us today ride in horse-drawn pungs—while wrapped in buffalo robes? Right from the beginning, it can be a bit difficult to empathize with Coffin's "paradise Christmas"—if only because the Maine he recalls seems not merely distant but perhaps a bit precious, too.

But I think that any careful reader of this essay will find that, lurking beneath the big-moon, crushed-diamond, sapphire-starred and apple-pudding world of Coffin's Maine, there are more complicated forces at work. From his affectionately recalled father, we hear the mournful song of Kitty Wells' lover, who swears off the banjo upon her poetic death. On the walk to Dragonfly Spring to fell a Christmas tree, we meet a frog frozen-still in the ice, suspended between the world of the living and the dead. Among the dubious Bible-speaking aunts of every complexion and cut, among the pipe-smoking uncles with their molasses taffy and abundant birch logs, among the cart-loads of cousins chomping on cookies, there haunts a feeling, still, that not everything in Coffin's world sings in perfect harmony.

By way of some distant Nantucket blood, and by fact of several debatable family stories, I know that I am somehow related to Coffin. In the house where I grew up in Brunswick, Maine, high on the top shelf of a cabinet, there sit a half-dozen volumes of Coffin's work, original printings signed to my grandparents and great-grandparents with notes of "cousinly" affection. Beneath some of those notes are small line drawings of winter landscapes:

white pines heavy with snow, stone houses tucked into snowy hillsides, their roofs heavy with snow and their stone chimneys puffing. Often, I have wondered if my writing gene were in fact a gift from the Uncle Robert I never knew. How nice it would have been to have him sitting in a rocking chair by the fireplace I never had, smoking quietly by my Christmas tree as I dozed off to sleep. And yet, based on his evocation of his Christmas, I sometimes wonder if the two of us would have had much to talk about.

Was Christmas for Coffin not tainted a bit by the complexity of the modern family? Did he not ride in that pung between the homes of divorced parents now and then? Did he not hear his friend's parents arguing over whether or not the family should attend midnight mass, in light of little Derek's recent encounter with atheism? My intention is not to be cynical or bitter here—rather, as Coffin's relative and as a fellow writer, I feel I have an obligation to hold the poet to the most important aesthetic measure: the test of time.

And in time, and from multiple and increasingly thoughtful readings of my little copy of *Christmas in Maine*—a copy which, as a 1941 first edition, is roughly the size of my smartphone—I have found some of the bridges I was looking for.

First, in the scene in which Coffin and his cousins innocently re-enact the battle of Gettysburg —a battle fought, quite importantly, by men who came from the Maine that Coffin knew so well. Perhaps that war was still on his mind, just as the Second World War, at roughly the time the book had been printed, was becoming an inevitable point on America's horizon. During my recent Christmases, one of the shadowy things on my mind that I tried, but failed, to ignore was the fact that the America of my generation, too, was not far from war—in fact, we had been in it for much of the last decade.

And second, what is clear to me after reading Coffin's work more than once is that Coffin, in an almost instinctive manner, seemed just as interested in the Christmas on his saltwater farm as he was in the nation at large. Coffin's Maine, even at Christmas, reflects an America deeply burdened by its own failures and inequalities and injustices. During my most recent Christmas, while my wife and I and our two daughters and all our big loving family members asked ourselves again how we might best remember the meaning of the season, it was suggested more than once that we could pray for the people in Ferguson, Missouri, and in New York, who wished for nothing more than to be heard, and to breathe.

I understand that the best ending is not always a big bright red bow, tied neatly around the perfectly wrapped gift. And I think Uncle Robert—he understood that, too. As his younger, remembered self wanders off into sleep on the last page of *Christmas in Maine*, the final image in his mind is not some snowy paradise of candy canes and crackling fires; rather, it is a vision of the battle of Big Bethel: the Milky Way of Yankee campfires the night before the fight, and the dawn of a new day and—there is no mistaking this—death. How does one go to sleep on this final morbid note that Coffin leaves us with? While many of us would prefer to meditate on the fullness of our bellies, on the days of vacation left before the New Year, Coffin assertively brings us instead to the old winds of the world and the cosmic motion of the bright stars. Lest we feel alone in this vision, he has already, pages ago, given us all the wisdom we need: "The

secret to the best Christmas," Coffin writes, shortly after describing the carving of the beloved family goose, "is everybody doing the same things, all at the same time."

Now, nearly seventy-five years since Uncle Robert first told this story, at least that much has remained the same.

JAED COFFIN
Brunswick, Maine
Winter 2015

Photo by Molly Haley

JAED COFFIN is the author of the memoir A Chant to Soothe Wild Elephants *and the forthcoming* Roughhouse Friday. *He lives in his hometown of Brunswick, Maine, with his wife and two daughters, and is an assistant professor of English at the University of New Hampshire. For more information about his work, please visit www.jaedcoffin.com.*

If you want to have a Christmas like the one we had on Paradise Farm when I was a boy, you will have to hunt up a salt-water farm on the Maine coast, with bays on both sides of it, and a road that goes around all sorts of bays, up over Misery Hill and down, and through the fir trees so close together that they brush you and your horse on both cheeks. That is the only kind of place a Christmas like that grows. You must have a clear December night, with blue Maine stars snapping like sapphires with the cold, and the big moon flooding full over Misery, and lighting up the snowy spruce boughs like crushed diamonds. You ought to be wrapped in a buffalo robe to your nose and be sitting in a family pung, and have your breath trailing along with you as you slide over the dry, whistling snow. You will have to sing the songs we sang, "God Rest Ye Merry, Gentlemen" and "Joy to the World," and you will be able to see your songs around you in the air like blue smoke. That's the only way to come to a Paradise Christmas.

And you really should cross over at least one broad bay on the ice, and feel the tide rifts bounce you as the runners slide over them. And if the whole bay booms out, every now and then, and the sound echoes around the wooded islands for miles, you will be having the sort of ride we loved to take from town, the night before Christmas.

I won't insist on your having a father like ours to drive you home to your Christmas. One with a wide moustache full of icicles, and eyes like the stars of the morning. That would be impossible, anyway, for there has been only one of him in the world. But it is too bad, just the same. For you won't have the stories we had by the fireplace. You won't hear about Kitty Wells who died beautifully in song just as the sun came over the tops of the eastern mountains and just after her lover had named the wedding day, and you will not hear how Kitty's departure put an end to his mastering the banjo:

> *But death came in my cabin door*
> *And took from me my joy, my pride,*
> *And when they said she was no more,*
> *I laid my banjo down and cried.*

But you will be able to have the rooms of the farmhouse banked with emerald jewels clustered on bayberry boughs, clumps of everlasting roses with gold spots in the middle of them, tree evergreens, and the evergreen that runs all over the Maine woods and every so often puts up a bunch of palm leaves. And there will be rose-hips stuck in pine boughs. And caraway seeds in every crust and cookie in place.

An aunt should be on hand, an aunt who believes in yarrow tea and the Bible as the two things needed to keep children well. She will read the Nativity story aloud to the family, hurrying over the really exciting parts that happened at the stable, and bearing down hard on what the angels had to say and the more edifying points that might be supposed to improve small boys who like to lie too long abed in the mornings. She will put a moral even into Christmas greens, and she will serve well as a counter-irritant to the overeating of mince pies. She will insist on all boys washing behind their ears, and that will keep her days full to the brim.

The Christmas tree will be there, and it will have a top so high that it will have to be bent over and run along the ceiling of the sitting room. It will be the best fir tree of the Paradise forests, picked from ten thousand almost perfect ones, and every bough on it will be like old-fashioned fans wide open. You will have brought it home that very morning, on the sled, from Dragonfly Spring.

Dragonfly Spring was frozen solid to the bottom, and you could look down into it and see the rainbows where you dented it with your copper-toed boots, see whole ferns caught motionless in the crystal deeps, and a frog, too, down there, with hands just like a baby's on him. Your small sister—the one with hair like new honey laid open in the middle of a honeycomb—had cried out, "Let's dig him up and take him home and warm his feet!" (She is the same sister who ate up all your more vivid pastel crayons when you were away at school, and then ate up all the things you had been pretty sure were toadstools in Bluejay Woods, when you were supposed to be keeping an eye on her, but were buried so deep in "Mosses from an Old Manse" that you couldn't have been dug up with horses and oxen.)

Your dog, Snoozer, who is a curious and intricate combination of many merry pugs and many mournful hound-dogs, was snuffling all the time, hot on the feather-stitching the mice had made from bush to bush while you were felling the Christmas tree. A red squirrel was taking a white-pine cone apart on a hemlock bough, and telling Snoozer what he thought of him and all other dogs, the hour or so you were there.

There will be a lot of aunts in the house besides the Biblical one. Aunts of every complexion and cut. Christmas is the one time that even the most dubious of aunts take on value. One of them can make up wreaths, another can make rock candy that puts a tremble on the heart, and still another can steer your twelve-seater bob-sled—and turn it over, bottom up, with you all in just the right place for a fine spill.

There will be uncles, too, to hold one end of the molasses taffy you will pull sooner or later, yanking it out till it flashes and turns into cornsilk that almost floats in the air, tossing your end of it back and probably lassoing your uncle around his neck as you do it, and pulling out a new rope of solid honey.

The uncles will smoke, too, and that will be a help to all the younger brothers who have been smoking their acorn-pipes out in the woodshed, and who don't want their breaths to give them away. The uncles will make themselves useful in other ways. They will rig up schooners no bigger than your thumb, with shrouds like cobwebs; they will mend the bob-sled, tie up cut fingers, and sew on buttons after you shin up to the cupola in the barn; and—if you get on the good side of them—they will saw you up so much birch wood that you won't have to lay hand to a bucksaw till after New Year's.

There will be cousins by the cart load. He-ones and she-ones. The size you can sit on, and the size that can sit on you. Enough for two armies, on Little Round Top and on Big, up in the haymow. You will play Gettysburg there till your heads are full of hay chaff that will keep six aunts busy cleaning it out. And then you will come into the house and down a whole crock of molasses cookies—the kind that go up in peaks in the middle— which somebody was foolish enough to leave the cover off.

Every holiday that came along, in my father's house, was the gathering of an Anglo-Saxon clan. My father was built for lots of people 'round him. But Christmas was a whole assembly of the West Saxons! My father wanted people in squads. There were men with wide moustaches and men with smooth places on top of their heads, women wide and narrow. Cousins of the second and third water, even, were there. Hired men, too. They were special guests and had to be handled with kid gloves, as New England hired men must. They had to have the best of everything, and you could not find fault with them, as you could with uncles, if they smacked you for upsetting their coffee into their laps. Babies were underfoot in full cry. The older children hunted in packs.

The table had to be pieced out with flour barrels and bread boards and ironing boards. It was a house's length from the head of the table, where your father sat and manufactured the roast up into slivers, to your mother dishing out the pork gravy. Whole geese disappeared on the way down. The Christmas cake, which had been left sweetly to itself for a month to age into a miracle, was a narrow isthmus when it got to Mother. But Mother always said that Christmas, to her, was watching other people eat. She was the kind of mother who claimed that the neck and the back of the chicken were the tastiest parts.

The prize goose, whom you had brought up by hand and called Oliver Cromwell, Old Ironsides, or some such distinguished title, was duly carved. And Father found his wishbone snow-white and you all applauded, for that meant lots of snow and two more months of coasting on your sleds. There were mince pies by the legion. And if Uncle Tom were there, a whole raccoon baked just for him and girt around with browned sweet potatoes. Mother's wild strawberry jam was there on deck, winking at you like rubies from the holes in tarts that melted away like bubbles in the mouth. That dinner was three hours in Beulah Land!

Of course, there will be an apple pudding at such a season. Steamed in a lard bucket, and cut open with a string. A sauce of oranges and lemons to make an ocean around each steaming volcano of suet and russet apples as it falls crumbling from the loop of twine. It will have to be steamed in the boiler, if your Christmas is to be the size of ours, and cooked in a ten-pound lard pail. Better use a cod line instead of the twine of other holidays, to parcel it out to the members of the clan.

The whole nation of you in the house will go from one thing to another. The secret of the best Christmases is everybody doing the same things all at the same time. You will all fall to and string cranberries and popcorn for the tree, and the bright lines each of you has a hold on will radiate from the tree like ribbons on a maypole. Everybody will have needles and thread in the mouth, you will all get in each other's way, but that is the art of doing Christmas right. You will all bundle up together for the ride in the afternoon. You had better take the horse-sled, as the pung will not begin to hold you. And even then a dozen or so of assorted uncles and aunts and cousins will have to come trooping after through the deep snow, and wait for their turn on the straw in the sled. Smaller cousins will fall off over the sides in great knots and never be missed, and the hullabaloo will roar on and send the rabbits flying away through the woods, showing their bobbing scuts.

Everybody will hang presents on the tree at once, when the sun has dipped down into the spruces in the west and you are back home in the sitting-room. There will be no nonsense of tiptoeing up and edging a package on when nobody is looking. Everybody knows who is giving him what. There is no mystery about it. Aunt Ella has made rag dinahs for all hands and the cook—for all under fourteen years of age—and she does not care who knows it. The dinahs are all alike, except that those for the children whose lower garments are forked have forked red-flannel pants instead of red-flannel petticoats. They all have pearl button eyes and stocking toes for faces. There will be so many hands at work on the tree at once that the whole thing will probably go over two or three times, and it will be well to make it fast with a hawser or so.

And then you will turn right around and take the presents off again, the minute you have got them all on and have lighted the candles up. There will be no waiting, with small children sitting around with aching hearts. The real candles will be a problem, in all that mass of spills. Boughs will take fire here and there. But there will be plenty of uncles around to crush out the small bonfires in their big brown hands. All the same, it would be well to have an uncle Thomas who can take up a live coal in his thumb and finger, and light his pipe from it, cool as a cucumber. Better turn the extinguishing of the tree over to him.

There will be boughten presents, to be sure—a turtle of cardboard in a glassed, dainty box, hung on springs and swimming for dear life with all four feet, and popguns with their barrels ringed and streaked with red and yellow lines. Why popguns should be painted like broomsticks is one of the mysteries, along with the blue paint you always find on Maine cartwheels. Somebody will probably get one of those Swiss music-boxes that will eke out a ghostly "Last Rose of Summer," if tenderly cranked. There should be those little bottles of transparent candies, with real syrup in them, which I used to live for through the years. And there must be a German doll for every last girl, with mountains of yellow hair and cheeks looking as if life were a continuous blowing of bubbles. Boughten things are all right.

But if it is going to be our kind of Christmas, most of the presents will
be home-made. Socks knit by the aunt who swears only by useful gifts.
You have seen those socks growing up from their white toes for the last two
weeks. Wristers, always red. A box of Aunt Louise's candied orange peel
that she will never let on to anybody how she makes. Your father will have
made a sled for every mother's son and daughter of you, with a bluebird,
or robin redbreast, more real than life, painted on each one and your name
underneath. You will never have another present to match that, though you
grow up and become Midases. Popcorn balls, big as muskmelons, will be
common ware. They will be dripping with molasses, and will stick your
wristers and socks and other treasures together.

But the pith of the party is not reached until the whole nation of you sits down in rocking chairs, or lies down on their bellies in front of the six-foot gulf of the fireplace. The presents are all stowed, heaped and tucked away, stuck fast with cornballs. The last lamps are out. The firelight dances on the ceiling.

All the babies will be hushed and put away. All the younger fry will be more than half asleep. The toasted cheese and red herring will go 'round. The herring, by the way,—if you are worthy to wear my shoes after me—which you yourself have smoked with green oak, and have gotten your two eyes so that they looked like two burnt holes in a blanket while doing it, and have hugely enjoyed every hour of it all.

Then you had best find a fair substitute for my father. Give him the best chair in the house—and the way to find that is to push the cat out of it—and let him tear! He will begin by telling you about such people as the brilliant young ladies of Philadelphia who had a piano too big to fit their house, so they put it on the porch and played on it through the open window. Then he will sit back and work his way to the Caliph of Bagdad, who had a daughter so homely that she had to wear a sack on her head when her suitors came awooing, and how she fell down a well and made herself a great fortune, and won the handsomest husband that ever wore a turban. That story, by the way, you will not find in the "Arabian Nights" even though you look for it, as I have done, till you have gray hairs in your head.

The firelight will get into your father's eyes and on his hair. He will move on from Bagdad to Big Bethel, and tell you all how the Yankee campfires looked like the high Milky Way itself all night long before the battle; how the dew silvered every sleeping soldier's face and the stacked rifles, as the dawn came up with the new day and death. And you will hug your knees and hear the wind outside going its rounds among the snowy pines, and you will listen on till the story you are hearing becomes a part of the old winds of the world and the motion of the bright stars.

And probably it will take two uncles at least
to carry you to bed.

About the Author

ROBERT PETER TRISTRAM COFFIN was born in 1892 in Brunswick, Maine. He attended Bowdoin College and Princeton University, and was also a Rhodes Scholar at Oxford University and served in the U.S. Army. He taught at Wells College in New York from 1921 to 1934 before returning to Bowdoin, where he was a Pierce Professor of English until his death in 1955. A prolific writer and popular speaker who drew inspiration from his time spent on a saltwater farm in Maine, he published more than three dozen works of prose and poetry. His book, *Strange Holiness*, won the 1936 Pulitzer Prize for Poetry.

About the Artist

BLUE BUTTERFIELD is a woodblock print artist who grew up in Bar Harbor and currently resides in Portland, Maine. She graduated from Bowdoin College and received her Masters in Health Professions from Northeastern University. She is known for her woodblock calendar "A Year in Maine," which she has produced annually since 2006. She has works in permanent collections in institutions across Maine. When not carving wood, she practices medicine as a physician assistant at Maine Medical Center. Her other devotions and hankerings include Masters Track and Field, absurd athletic competitions, and making Portland-inspired woodblock t-shirts for her husband and two sons.